"I Don't like Space Glop!"

OTHER TITLES IN THE SAME SERIES

"Og Fo" says the Space Bug
0 7475 3929 4 (hbk)
0 7475 3562 0 (pbk)

When a naughty space bug called Zug Zug meets a mad
dog called Pat, there is sure to be trouble. Especially
when there is a fountain to fall in.

"Do I Look Funny to You?"
0 7475 3930 8 (hbk)
0 7475 3561 2 (pbk)

Jazz is just a normal space girl and she wants to go to
school with Max to join in earth lessons. But everyone
she meets keeps laughing at her and they haven't even
seen Zug Zug – or have they?

Pets Just Want to Have Fun
0 7475 3931 6 (hbk)
0 7475 3560 4 (pbk)

Max and Jazz are going to the shops to buy something
for tea. But their pets are causing trouble everywhere
they go. Oh, no, what will Mum say!

"I Don't like Space Glop!"

NICOLA MATTHEWS

Illustrated by
Eleanor Taylor

BLOOMSBURY
CHILDREN'S
BOOKS

First published in Great Britain in 1998
Bloomsbury Publishing Plc, 38 Soho Square, London, W1V 5DF

ISBN 0 7475 3932 4 (hardback)
ISBN 0 7475 3563 9 (paperback)

Printed in England by Clays Ltd, St Ives plc

10 9 8 7 6 5 4 3 2 1

Contents

Introduction

Learning to read with phonics is now recognised as one of the best ways in which a child can gain reading skills. The phonic system is not only used in most primary schools, but is also a method of teaching encouraged by the government, who recognise that the phonics method is a reliable and thorough way to teach reading.

Created to compliment phonic reading in schools, this book is perfect for home reading. In its pages the young reader will find all the excitement and action they could want, – as Max and Jazz, Zug Zug and Pat, enjoy madcap adventures with lots of fun and humour. Most importantly, the exciting story-line with controlled phonic vocabulary, will ensure that the beginner reader will soon be reading with confidence.

Chapter One

Jazz is sad. The space ship is a mess. Jazz is a space kid, and space kids do not like to live in a mess.

Zug Zug, the space bug, likes space slugs and frogs. He lets them live in Jazz's clock – but they never stay in the clock.

The frogs jump around the space ship with muddy feet. The slugs leave slime all over the rug and all over Jazz's seats.

It is not easy to clean up mud, but Jazz can do it. It is

not easy to clean up slime, but
Jazz can do that too. It is not
easy to catch jumping frogs
and slimy slugs, but Jazz gets
her net and jumps around after

them. She puts them back inside
the clock and closes the door
tight.

Zug Zug, the space bug, is a
very messy eater. He drops
space glop on Jazz's bed. Space

glop is green and very smelly.
He blobs red jam on Jazz's best
space rug. Jazz does not want
space glop on her bed or red
jam on her space rug.

So she gets her brush and

pan and her yellow duster. She gets rid of the red jam but can't get rid of the space glop. Jazz is sad because of the space glop. She is sad and grumpy.

'Ob glob dob dab, Jazz?' says Zug Zug. 'What is the problem, Jazz?'

'This place is a mess,' said Jazz. 'And we have run out of space vim. I need space vim to get rid of space glop.'

'Ig big tig jig jug,' says Zug Zug. 'I like space glop in my bed.'

'Well, I don't!' says Jazz.

'We'll have to go to planet Igg to get some vim and that's that.'

'Gag dag pog Pat, ag gax Max?' says Zug Zug. 'Can we take Pat and Max?'

'OK,' says Jazz, cheering up a bit. 'That would be fun. Let's go and pick them up in the space ship. Then we can go to planet Igg to get some space vim.'

Jazz gets in her seat and straps on her seat belt. Zug Zug gets in his seat and straps on his seat belt.

'Ready for lift off. Flip the switch, Zug Zug!' says Jazz.

'Og fo!' says Zug Zug. 'Oh no!'

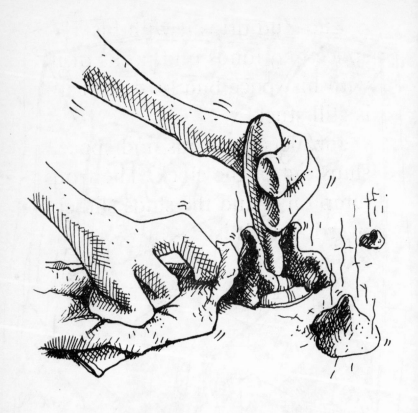

The switch will not flip! There
is glop on the switch and it is
stuck. Jazz unstraps her belt
and gets her yellow duster. She
rubs at the switch and scrubs at
it, but it is still stuck!

Zug Zug grips it with his space bug fangs and pecks at it with his space bug beak, but it is still stuck!

Jazz lets the frogs and space slugs out of the clock. The frogs jump on it and the slugs slither over it, but it is still stuck!

'Well,' says Jazz, 'we will just have to leave the space ship here and go in the blast box instead.'

The blast box is Jazz's invention. It does not work very well.

'Og fo!' says Zug Zug. 'Oh, no!'

Chapter Two

'OK, let's Go!' says Jazz.
She shuts her eyes and thinks
about Max's house. That's how
the blast box works. It goes
wherever Jazz wants it to.

The blast box starts to shake.
The blast box starts to rattle.

The blast box starts to wobble and – **ZOOM**! The blast box blasts away – and lands with a crash in Max's shed.

'Ag dag rag zot!' says Zug Zug crossly. 'That was a bad landing!'

Zug Zug gets up from the floor and shakes his wings.

'Ap gap bop bop!' he says. 'I do not like this blast box and you are a bad driver!'

Jazz does not hear him. She gets out of the blast box and looks round.

'This does not look like Max's house,' she says.

Zug Zug gets out too. 'Rig

dig brig,' he says. 'It does not look like anything. It's too dark!'

Jazz says, 'It does not sound like Max's house. I cannot hear Mum shouting or Pat yapping.'

'Bin hin Max nax!' says Zug
Zug. 'That's because it isn't
Max's house. It's a shed!'

'Oh no!' says Jazz.

'Og yen!' says Zug Zug. 'Oh
yes!'

'Woof! Woof!' Jazz and Zug
Zug can hear Pat outside.
'Bum! Pat!' yells Zug Zug.
'Help! Pat!'

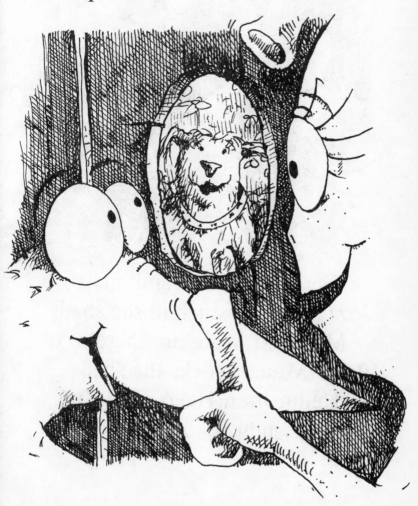

'Get Max and Mum!' yells
Jazz. 'We are stuck in the shed!'

Max and Mum are there in a
flash. Mum unlocks the shed.

'Hello, Jazz. Hello, Zug Zug.
Why are you in the shed?' she
says.

Jazz tells Mum about the
blast box, but Mum does not
hear. She can see that Pat is
digging up her flower beds and
she runs off to save her flowers.

Jazz tells Max about the trip
to space.

Max asks Mum, 'Mum, please may I go with Jazz? She needs to get some things to clean up the space ship.'

Mum does not know he
wants to go to space in a blast
box.

'OK, but don't be too long,'
she says. She is pleased that he
will have something to do.

'That mad dog can go with you
too. I do not want him in my
garden. Goodbye and be good!'
Mum is busy. She doesn't see

Max, Zug Zug, Pat and Jazz
go into the shed. She doesn't
see them go into the blast box.
She doesn't hear Zug Zug say,

'Og fo!' and Jazz say, 'Let's go!'
    Maybe that's a good thing!

Chapter Three

The blast box is not very big. It
is a squash to get them all in.
Zug Zug has to sit on Jazz's
head and Pat has to sit on
Max's lap.

'OK, let's go!' says Jazz. She
shuts her eyes and thinks about

the planet Igg where the space
vim is.

The blast box starts to shake.
The blast box starts to rattle.
The blast box starts to wobble
and – ZOOM!
The blast box blasts

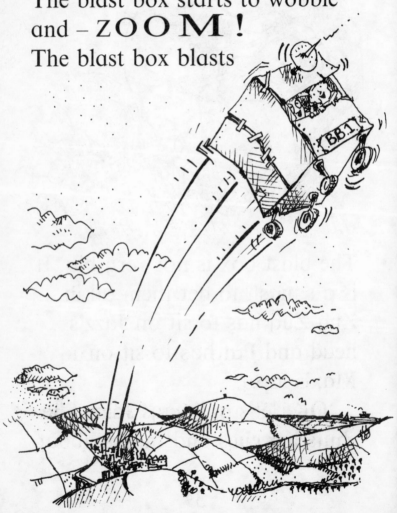

away and lands with a crash on
Igg.

'Ag dag rag zot!' says Zug
Zug crossly.

'Ouch!' says Max. 'What did
Zug Zug say?'

'He thinks it was a bad landing,' says Jazz.

'I know what he means,' says Max.

'Woof!' says Pat.

'You do all make a fuss,' says Jazz. 'Let's go and get the space vim.'

The blast box has landed near a lot of trees. They are all blue with yellow flowers. They look like footballs. The flowers smell like sweets. The grass is like pink candy floss and smells of sweets too.

'I like this place,' says Max.

Jazz gets some yellow flowers from the trees and puts them in her bag. Pat and Zug Zug are chasing a yellow football

flower. Zug Zug heads the ball and Pat chases it and gets it in her jaws.

'Don't do that!' yells Jazz, but it is too late. The yellow

football flower bursts with a
loud pop. Yellow gunk jets into
the air and all over Pat and
Zug Zug.

'Vig pag vog dag!' says Zug
Zug.

'Yuk!' Pat yelps.

Now the pets are all yellow and slimy. They look like they have been dipped in cold yellow custard.

'What is that?' asks Max.

'That,' says Jazz, 'is space

vim. It is the stickiest stuff in
space. That is why it gets rid of
space glop. Even space glop
sticks to space vim. We'd better
get back to the blast box fast or
Pat and Zug Zug will stick to
the grass here.'

The slimy pets get into the
blast box. Jazz and Max get
into the blast box. They do not
want to get near the pets but
the blast box is not
very big.

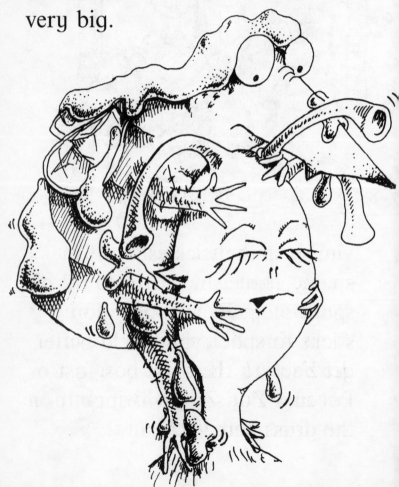

'Let's go before we all stick
to each other,' says Jazz.

She shuts her eyes and thinks
of the space ship. It is not easy
because space vim is dripping
from Zug Zug's wings down
Jazz's neck. It is not easy
because Pat's tail is dripping on
her foot. But Jazz can do it.

The blast box starts to shake.
The blast box starts to rattle.
The blast box starts to wobble
and – ZOOM!
The blast box blasts away –
and lands with a crash in Jazz's
space ship.

Chapter Four

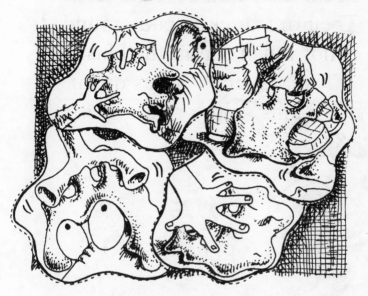

The blast box lands but Jazz doesn't get out. She can't get out.

Jazz is stuck to Zug Zug. Zug Zug is stuck to Pat. Pat is stuck to Max and Max is stuck to the blast box.

'Og fo!' says Zug Zug.

'What do we do now?' says
Max. He cannot lift his feet.
They are stuck to the ground. It
is not much fun in the blast

box. Jazz had not told them
that space vim smells like a
stink bomb.

'Bin dop fop, Jazz,' says Zug
Zug. 'Now is a good time for a
plan, Jazz.'

Jazz grins. 'I have a plan but I don't think you will like it.'

Jazz shuts her eyes and thinks . . . she thinks of the pond in the park.

The blast box starts to shake.

The blast box starts to rattle.
The blast box starts to wobble
and – ZOOM!
   The blast box blasts away –
and lands with a splash in the
pond. Max yells. Pat yelps and

Zug Zug shouts. The pond is
cold. They did not expect Jazz
to do that!

Space vim is not sticky when

it is wet. Now Jazz is not stuck
to Zug Zug. Zug Zug is not
stuck to Pat. Pat is not stuck to
Max and Max's feet are not

stuck to the blast box. Jazz
opens the blast box and they all
climb out.

Zug Zug is cross. Max is cold
and grumpy. Then Pat shakes
herself and Max gets even
wetter.

'Jazz, that was a bad idea!' he says.

'It was a bad idea,' says Jazz. 'I have only three space vim flowers left in my bag and my blast box has sunk to the

57

bottom of the pond and I still
have to clean up the space
ship.'

Jazz and Max, Zug Zug and
Pat all walk back to the space

ship. It is a long walk. Jazz is sad.

'I have broken my blast box. It will never blast again now, and I will have to walk

everywhere. After all that this
ship is still a mess. I am fed up,'
she says.

Max looks round. 'It is a
mess. but we'll help clean up,
Jazz,' says Max.

Jazz gets out the space vim

flowers. Max gets the brush.
Pat puts a duster on her tail.
Even Zug Zug holds the dust
pan in his beak. Soon the space
ship is as clean as a new pin.
Jazz is very happy.

'Brig nig pop,' says Zug
Zug. That means,
'Why don't you
turn that awful
blast box into a
cleaning
machine?'

'That's a good idea! A very good idea!' says Jazz. 'Let's go and get it from the pond! Zug Zug, don't run away. I need you. I have a plan . . .'

'Og fo!' says Zug Zug. 'Og fo!'

OTHER YOUNG FICTION SERIES

BEST PETS:
Timmy and Tiger 0 7475 3878 6 (hbk) /3564 7 (pbk)
Gita and Goldie 0 7475 3879 4 (hbk) /3656 5 (pbk)
Becky and Beauty 0 7475 3880 8 (hbk) /3566 3 (pbk)
Paul and Percy 0 7475 3881 6 (hbk) /3567 1 (pbk)

Your pet can be your best friend. Your pet will be loyal to
you, and look out for you. Sometimes your pet can even
save you from danger . . . In these heartwarming stories,
Tiger the cat, Goldie the dog, Beauty the pony and Percy
the parrot, prove that they really are best pets!

THE TIGERS:
Ghost Goalie 0 7475 3925 1 (hbk) /3846 8 (pbk)
Save the Pitch 0 7475 3926 X (hbk) /3847 6 (pbk)
The Terrible Trainer 0 7475 3927 8 (hbk) /3850 6 (pbk)
The Cup Final 0 7475 3928 6 (hbk) /3851 4 (pbk)

**"We're the Tigers . . . Hear us roar.
Seven-nil will be the score!"**

The Tigers are the best under-ten football team around –
and they know it. The preamble is always unpredictable,
but they have fun facing each new challenge with
unbridled enthusiasm and always win in the end – even if
it is a close run thing!